For Ozzy and Bo,
and all the adventures
they'll share together - S.L.

ORCHARD BOOKS
338 Euston Road, London NW1 3BH
Orchard Books Australia
Level 17/207 Kent Street, Sydney, NSW 2000
First published in 2013 by Orchard Books
ISBN 978 1 84616 943 4
Text and illustrations © Sam Lloyd 2013
The right of Sam Lloyd to be identified as the author
and illustrator of this book has been asserted by her in
accordance with the Copyright, Designs and Patents Act, 1988.
A CIP catalogue record for this book is available
from the British Library.
1 3 5 7 9 10 8 6 4 2
Printed in China
Orchard Books is a division of
Hachette Children's Books,
an Hachette UK company.
www.hachette.co.uk

Two Little Aliens

Sam Lloyd

ORCHARD

Wow!

Stop the rocket!
We haven't been here before.
It looks like fun!

Come on! Let's play!

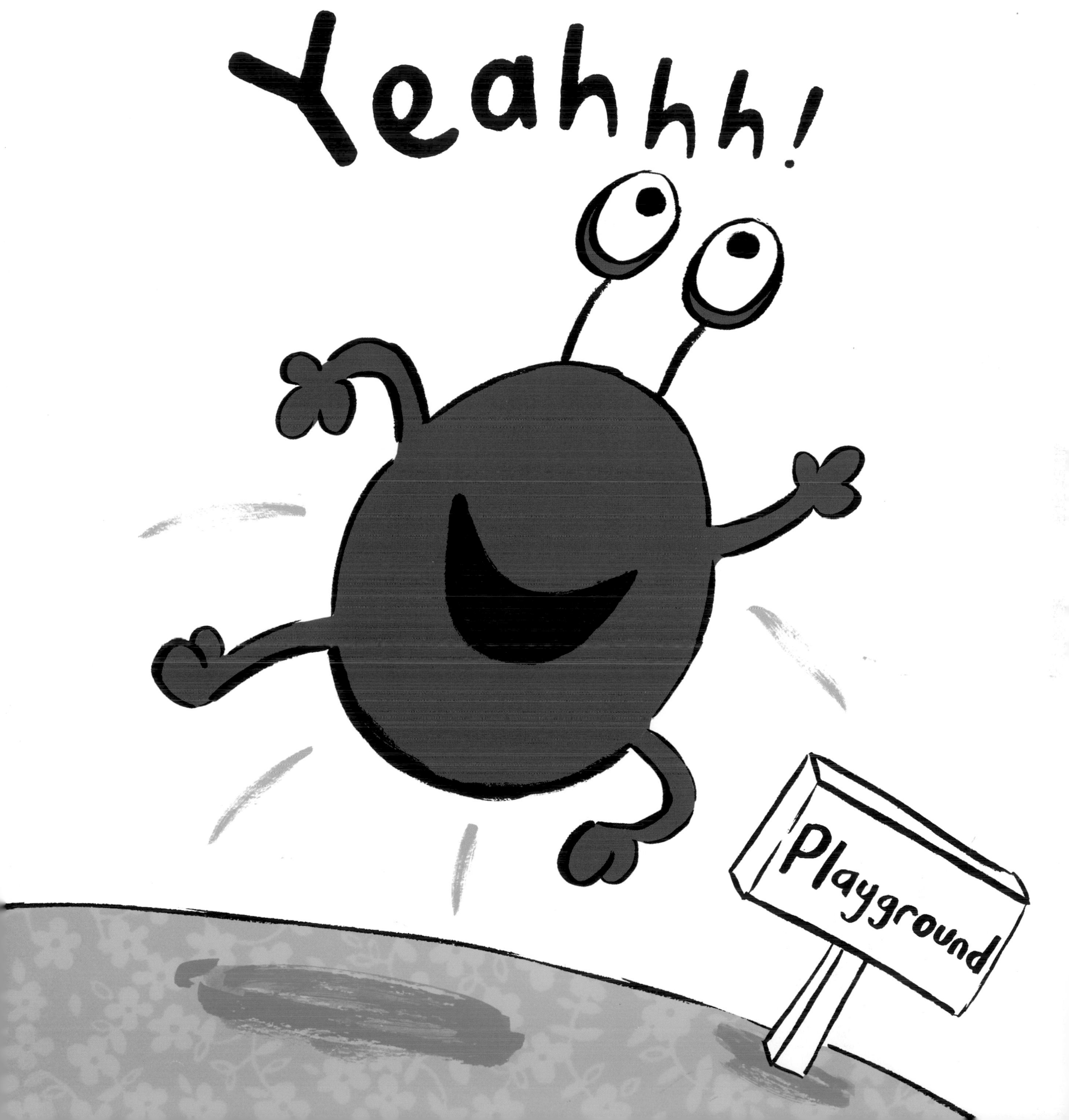
Yeahhh!
Playground

These things aren't for throwing.

We don't know what to do!

Oooh!

They look friendly.
Will they help us?

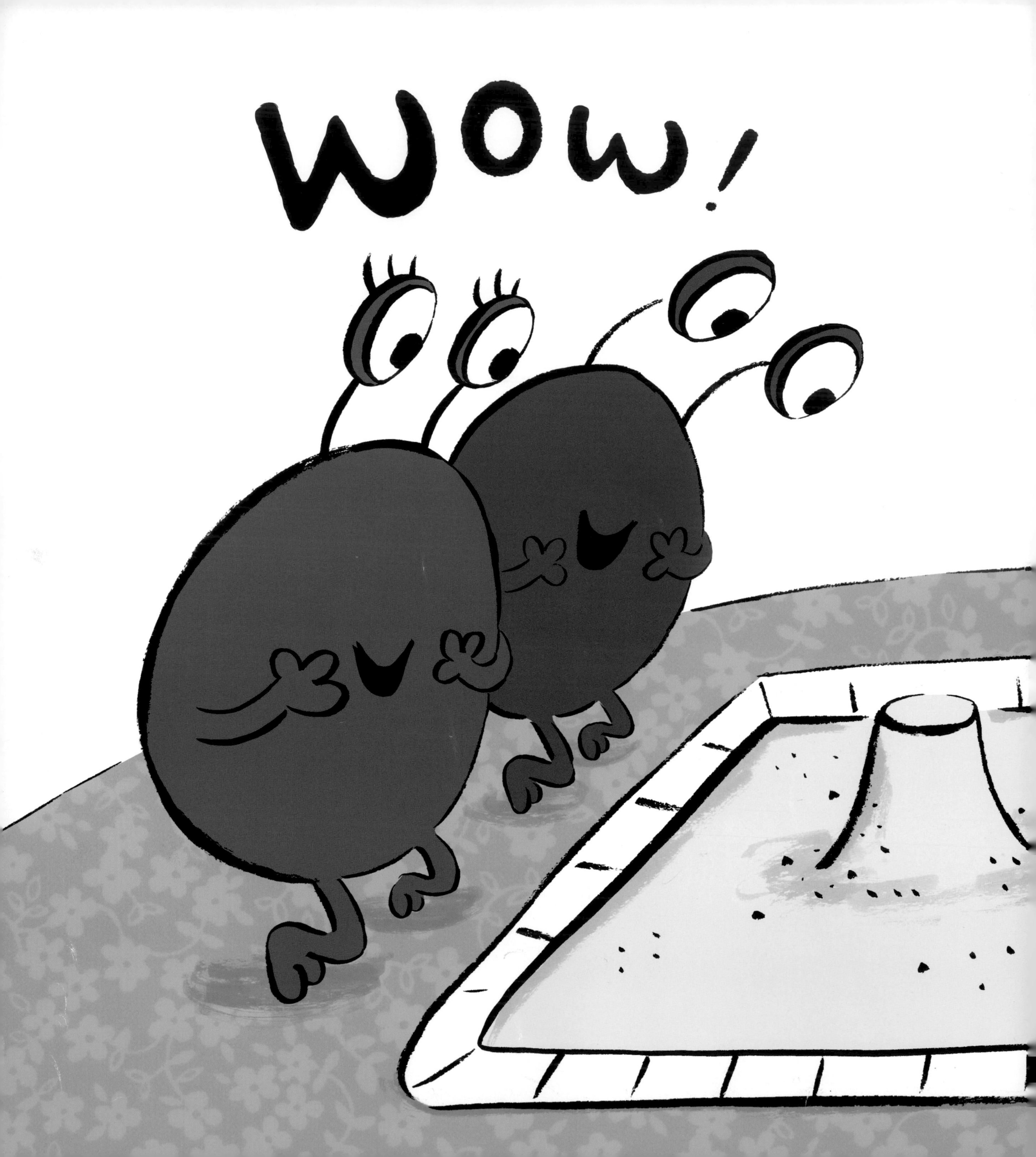
WOW!

This yellow stuff
makes shapes!

These things are for eating. They're yummy!

Wheee!

And this botty bouncer
is the best!

Aaah!

Thank you.
We've had so much fun.

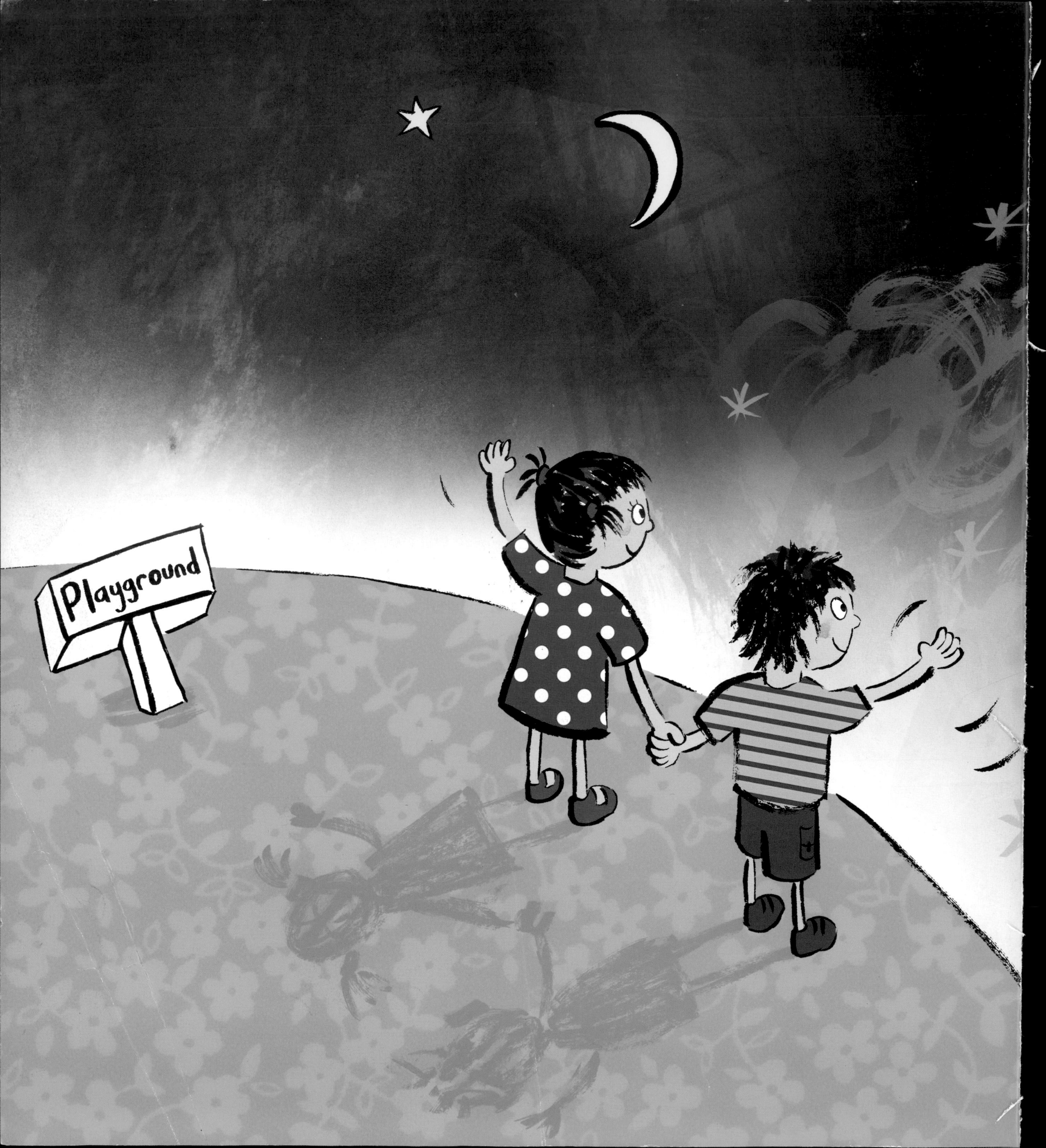
Playground

It's time for home.
We'll be back soon.

Bye bye!